Little
Monster
Did It!

HELEN COOPER

PUFFIN BOOKS

PUFFIN BOOKS
Published by the Penguin Group
Penguin Putnam Books for Young Readers,
345 Hudson Street, New York, NY 10014, U.S.A.
Penguin Books Ltd, 27 Wrights Lane, London W8 5TZ, England
Penguin Books Australia Ltd, Ringwood, Victoria, Australia
Penguin Books Canada Ltd, 10 Alcorn Avenue, Toronto, Ontario, Canada M4V 3B2
Penguin Books (N.Z.) Ltd, 182-190 Wairau Road, Auckland 10, New Zealand

Penguin Books Ltd, Registered Offices: Harmondsworth, Middlesex, England

First published in the United States of America by
Dial Books for Young Readers, a division of Penguin Books USA Inc., 1996
Published in Great Britain by Doubleday, a division of Transworld Publishers Ltd.
Published by Puffin Books, a member of Penguin Putnam Books for Young Readers, 1999

1 3 5 7 9 10 8 6 4 2

THE LIBRARY OF CONGRESS HAS CATALOGED THE DIAL EDITION AS FOLLOWS:
Cooper, Helen (Helen F.)
Little monster did it! / Helen Cooper—1st ed.
p.   cm.
"Published in Great Britain by Doubleday"—T.p. verso.
Summary: A small girl's favorite plush toy seems to be responsible for the mischievous
"accidents" that begin occurring when a new baby brother joins the household.
ISBN 0-8037-1993-0
[1. Jealousy—Fiction. 2. Babies—Fiction. 3. Family life—Fiction.] I. Title
PZ7.C78555Li 1996 [E]—dc20 95-30613 CIP AC

Puffin Books ISBN 0-14-055883-7
Printed in Mexico

The artwork for this book was prepared with watercolor paints.
It was then color-separated and reproduced in full color.

I liked it best with just us three,
only Mom and Dad and me.
It was quiet in our house . . .

most of the time.

Then one day Mom had to go to the
hospital. Before she left,
she gave me a present.

It had a tag on it.
The tag said:

Dear Amy,
This little
monster wants
to be your
friend.
xxxx Mom

I loved him right away, and he loved me too.

But he didn't love what Mom
brought home from the hospit[a]

Mom was all happy and smiling.
"Come and meet your little brother,"
she said. "Isn't he sweet?"

"I guess so," I said.
Little Monster didn't say anything.

Dad showed us
how to change diapers.

But Little Monster had
an accident . . .

and the diaper was really stinky . . .   so we left.

Later Mom tried to read us a story.

But Little Monster wouldn't sit still.
Then the baby started crying . . .
and there wasn't enough room for me anyway.

So Little Monster and I went upstairs
and pretended we were elephants.

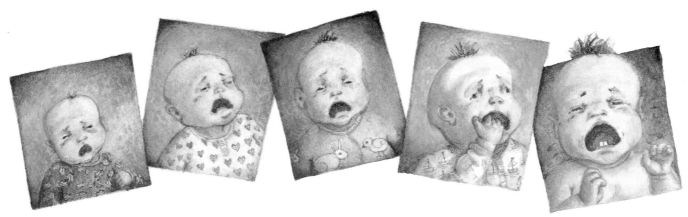

The baby cried a lot. For weeks
and weeks it wouldn't sleep at night.

The noise went on all winter.
It gave Little Monster bad dreams.

Some nights we both had bad dreams . . .

so we snuck into bed
with Mom and Dad.

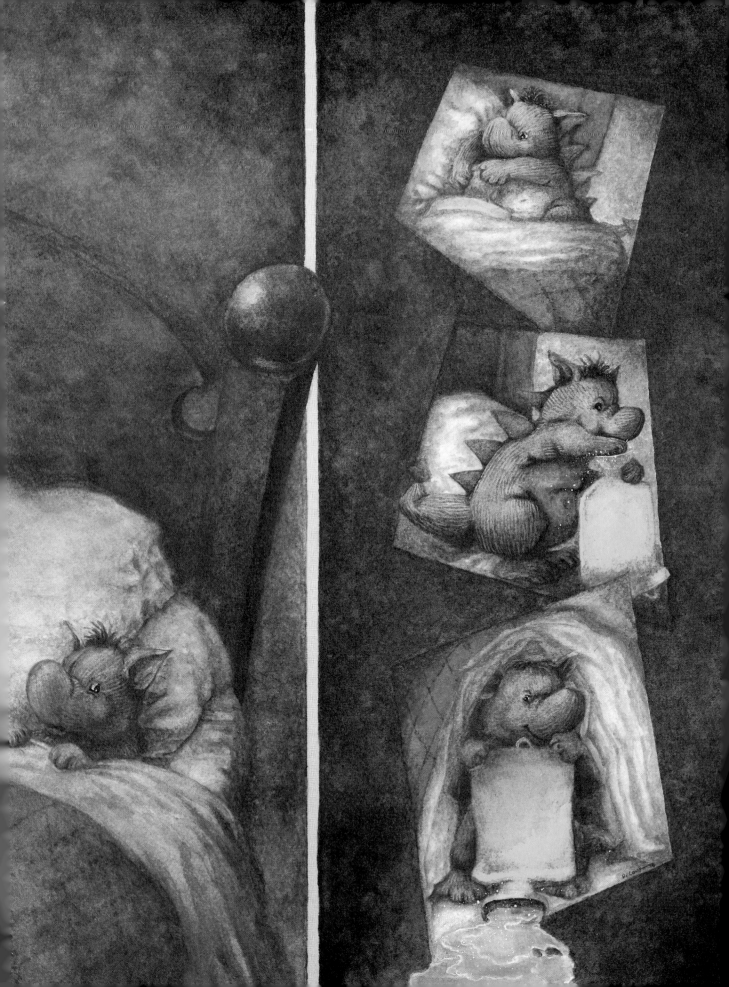

One night the bed got really wet.
It was from the hot water bottle.

"How did that happen?" asked Dad.
"Little Monster must have done it," I said.

"That's not funny," said Dad.
"Sleep in your own room if you can't be good."

But Little Monster
didn't want to be good there either.

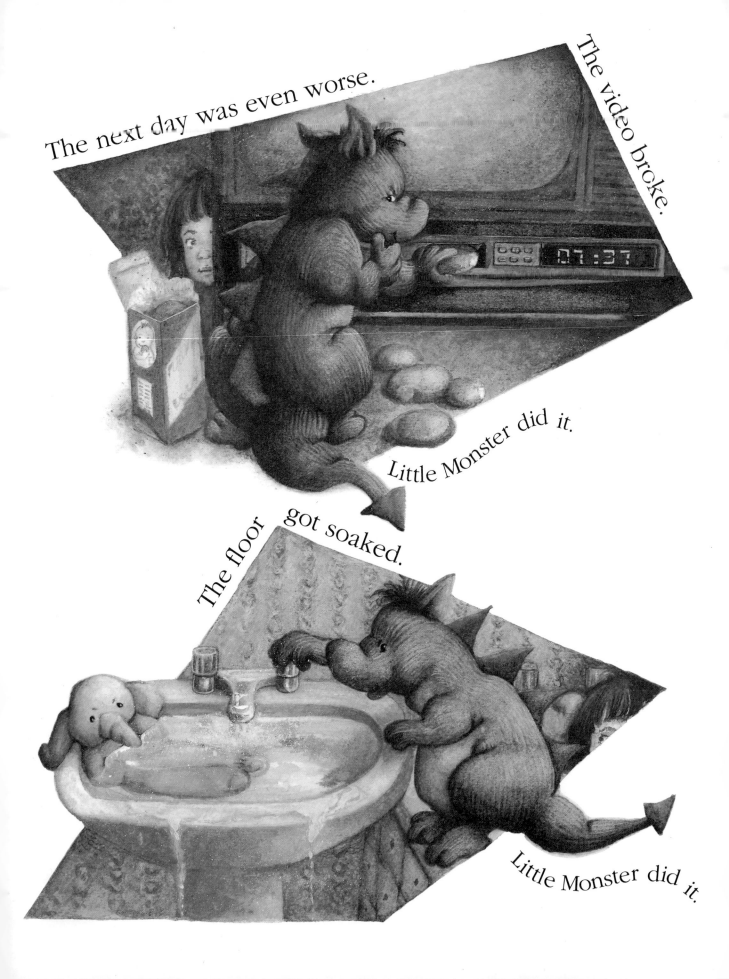

The next day was even worse. The video broke.

Little Monster did it.

The floor got soaked.

Little Monster did it.

The baby woke.

Little Monster did it.

"Behave yourself," yelled Dad,
"or Little Monster will have to go!"
"NO!" I shouted.

We ran downstairs
and pretended we were orphans.

That night Mom said we should try
being friends with the baby.
But Little Monster wouldn't.

"Can't we send the baby back?" I asked.
But Mom said we couldn't.
"He needs all of us to take care of him," she said.
"What would he do without us?"

What would he do without us?
I thought about it. . . .

Then I decided to help
him dry his toes.

And I told him a story
until he went to sleep.

But Little Monster didn't like it.
He dragged me off to bed.

When I
woke up
the next
morning,
Little Monster
was missing.
I went
downstairs
with Mom and Dad
and we found him . . .

in the kitchen.
"Enough is enough!"
shouted Mom.
"Get rid of that monster!
Right now!"

"NO!"

I cried.
Little Monster fell
into my arms and we ran.

But where could we hide?

Not in the toy box!
There was only one safe place. . . .

Mom and Dad caught up with us.

They looked at me and my baby brother.

They looked at Little Monster.

They looked at each other . . .

and they smiled.

We went downstairs then, just us three.
Dad made two cups of tea and
poured juice for me.
Mom said Little Monster could stay.
I said my brother could too.
"Now we'll have some peace and quiet
again, won't we?" asked Dad.
Maybe we will. . . .

I'll have to ask Little Monster.